The Big Animal Mix-Up
First published in hardback in 2011
First published in paperback in 2012

Text copyright © Gareth Edwards 2011
Illustrations copyright © Kanako Usui 2011

Hodder Children's Books, 338 Euston Road, London, NW1 3BH
Hodder Children's Books Australia, Level 17/207 Kent Street, Sydney, NSW 2000

The right of Gareth Edwards to be identified as the author and
Kanako Usui as the illustrator of this Work has been asserted
by them in accordance with the Copyright, Designs and Patent Act 1988.

PB ISBN: 978 0 340 98989 0

Printed in China

Hodder Children's Books is a division of Hachette Children's Books.
An Hachette UK Company.

www.hachette.co.uk

The Big Animal Mix-Up

Gareth Edwards
Kanako Usui

Hodder
Children's
Books

A division of Hachette Children's Books

"Hello Little Bear!
Here's a story for you
That's all about animals
And what they can do.

Look very carefully
And please let me know
If you spot any little
Mistakes as we go.

This is a **fish**.
It has very soft fur.
If you give it a cuddle
You'll hear it go 'purr'."

"Hang on a minute!

A fish can't do that.

If it's purry and furry,

It must be a...

"This is a cat.
It flies in the air.
There are eggs in its nest.
It has feathers, not hair."

"Hang on
a minute!

That's **not** the right word.
If it's covered in feathers,

It **must** be a...

"Here is a **bird**.
It slithers around,
And slides through the jungle
With a soft **hissing** sound."

"Hang on a minute!

You made a mistake.

If it hisses and slithers

It must be a...

"This is a snake
As tall as you please,
Its neck reaches up
To the tops of the trees."

...GIRAFFE!"

"Hang on
a minute!

You're making me laugh.

If it's got a long neck,

It must be a...

"This is a giraffe.

It likes cheese and it's small,

It squeaks and its house

Is a hole in the wall."

...MOUSE!"

"Hang on a minute!

A hole for a house?
If it squeaks
and eats cheese,

It must be a...

"Here is a mouse.
It swims in the sea
With a huge splashy tail.
It eats plankton for tea!"

"Hang on a minute!

A **huge** splashy tail?
If it swims and
eats plankton,

It **must** be a...

"This is a **whale**.
Its Pyjamas are red.
It's holding its bunny
And going to bed!"

...LITTLE BEAR!"

"Hang on a minute!

Just hold it right there.

If it's wearing pyjamas,

It must be...

"Well, I'm glad you could help me.
Now I have to go.
So it's time that I wished you
A friendly 'Hello'."

"Hang on a minute!

That still isn't right.
I'm going to sleep,

so it should be...

Other great Hodder picture books perfect to share with children:

978 0 340 98868 8

978 0 340 97037 9

978 0 340 98991 3

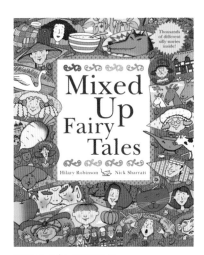

978 0 340 87558 2

978 0 340 98948 7

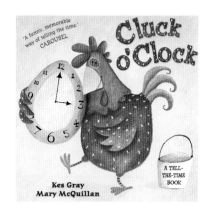

978 1 4449 0013 2